This book belongs to

_____

Given by

_____

Date

_____

Heaven Is ...

Lofty Thoughts for Little People

by Linda DeYmaz

Illustrated by Sabrina Smith

HEAVEN IS
published by
Little People Books
a division of Vision House Publishing
1217 NE Burnside, Suite 403
Gresham, Oregon 97030

© 1996 by Linda DeYmaz
Illustrations © 1996 by Sabrina Smith

International Standard Book Number 1-885305-48-6

96 97 98 99 00 01 02 03 04 05 - 10 9 8 7 6 5 4 3 2 1

This book is dedicated to our children ...

Zachary and Emily

You have taught me so much of the innocence of Heaven.
May you always long for your eternal home.

Linda

Madison Victoria

You are my little piece of Heaven on earth.

Sabrina

Heaven is God's home high
above the clouds.
Someday an angel will
take you there!

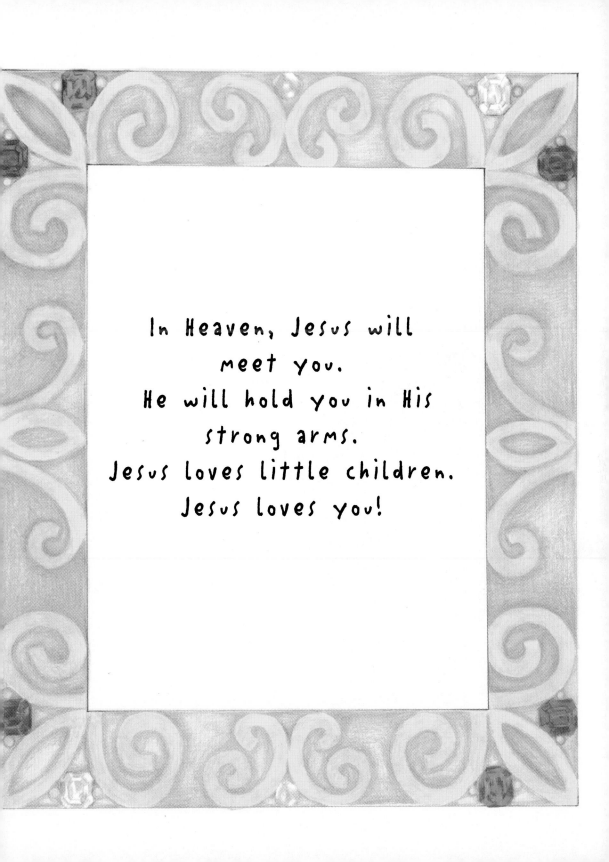

In Heaven, Jesus will
meet you.
He will hold you in His
strong arms.
Jesus loves little children.
Jesus loves you!

Heaven is beautiful.
Did you know the streets
are made of gold?
Real gold!
What do you think it will be like
to walk on streets of gold?

In Heaven, you will have
lots of friends.
You will run, giggle and laugh.
There are so many
fun places to play!

Heaven is a happy place.
When you fall
it won't hurt!
There are no tears
in Heaven.

Noah lives in Heaven.
Someday, he can tell you the story
of his big boat,
all the animals, and the very
first rainbow.
Would you like to meet Noah?

Heaven is wonderful
and there are
lots of parties.
You might even find
streamers and hats
and the best chocolate
cake ever!

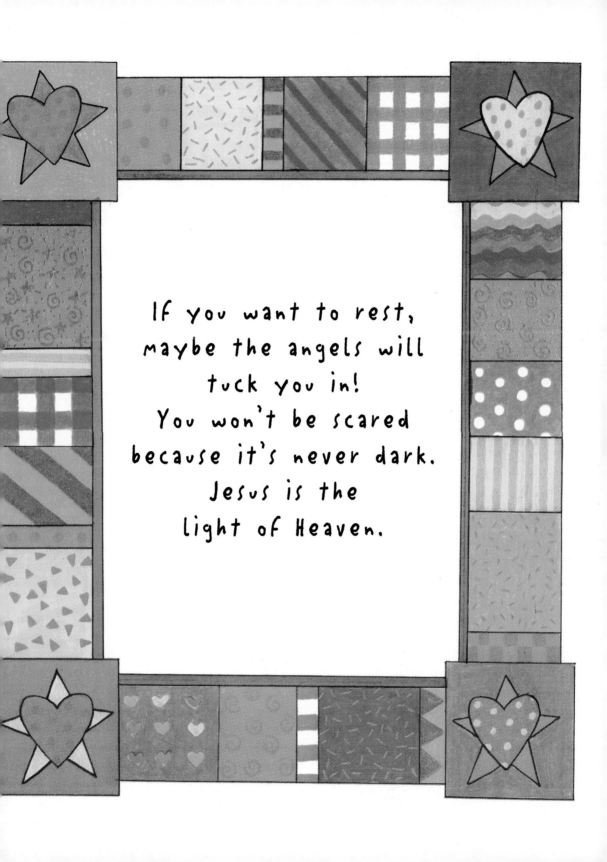

If you want to rest,
maybe the angels will
tuck you in!
You won't be scared
because it's never dark.
Jesus is the
light of Heaven.

Heaven is filled
with joy.
The angels are
always singing.
Someday, you can sing
with the angels!
What songs would you
like to sing in
Heaven?

Jezuz lovez me this I Krow for the Bible tellz me zo...

There is a river in the most
beautiful garden, and a big tree
with lots of yummy fruit.
The angels call it the tree of life.
How fun it will be to
live in Heaven!

Heaven is the city of God.
Sometime when you're all alone,
Look up into the sky
and imagine that you're there.

God has given you
special people to help
you learn about heaven.
Who can you ask to
tell you more?

Heaven is a place
made for you.
One day, would you
like to go there?

A Bit About Heaven ...

Heaven ... such a lofty concept for little ones. Yet our children have a unique way of combining innocence, excitement, and faith when talking about Heaven.

Is there any concept so inviting and at the same time so incomprehensible? There are so many questions! Where is Heaven? What's it like? Who will be there? Will we know one another? And, just what will we do there for all eternity?

Although all of our questions cannot be answered now, it's surprising how specific the Bible is about Heaven. Jesus taught His followers to pray, *"Our Father in Heaven...."* From this we learn that Heaven is a real place and that God is there. The Bible also tells us that Heaven was created by God, and it is a place of light, hope, and rewards.

One of the most intriguing thoughts about Heaven is that Jesus said, *"I go to pre-pare a place for you."* Now, the Bible says it took God just six days to create this world—beautiful coastlines, breath-taking mountain peaks, and rolling hills. So imag-ine how incredible Heaven must be since Jesus has been preparing it for nearly 2000 years! Truly, *no mere man has ever seen, heard or even imagined what won-derful things God has ready for those who love the Lord.*

This book was created as a tool to help you interact with your child about Heaven. Young children can understand simple concepts about Heaven and make choices concerning their eternal destiny. With these thoughts in mind, I pray this book will help them desire Heaven for their eternal home.

With love,

Linda

Helping Your Child Choose Jesus

The last question in the book gives you an opportunity
to begin teaching your child about Jesus.
Once your child is old enough to ask questions
concerning eternal life and salvation,
you can use this simple prayer of faith to help your child choose Jesus.

Dear Jesus,
Thank you for loving me.
I want to go to Heaven someday.
I want You to be my Savior and friend.
Please forgive me
for sometimes doing bad things,
and help me to do good things.
I love you Jesus!
Amen

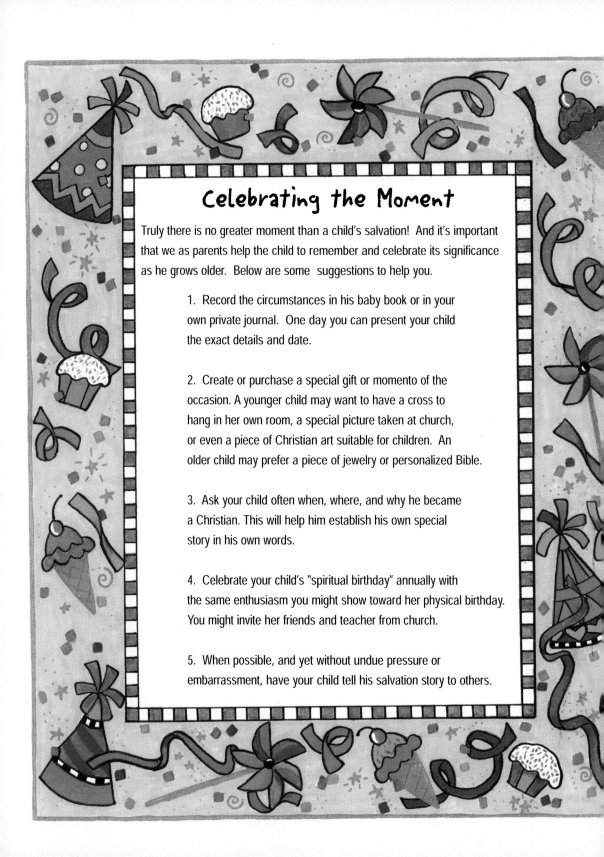

Celebrating the Moment

Truly there is no greater moment than a child's salvation! And it's important that we as parents help the child to remember and celebrate its significance as he grows older. Below are some suggestions to help you.

1. Record the circumstances in his baby book or in your own private journal. One day you can present your child the exact details and date.

2. Create or purchase a special gift or momento of the occasion. A younger child may want to have a cross to hang in her own room, a special picture taken at church, or even a piece of Christian art suitable for children. An older child may prefer a piece of jewelry or personalized Bible.

3. Ask your child often when, where, and why he became a Christian. This will help him establish his own special story in his own words.

4. Celebrate your child's "spiritual birthday" annually with the same enthusiasm you might show toward her physical birthday. You might invite her friends and teacher from church.

5. When possible, and yet without undue pressure or embarrassment, have your child tell his salvation story to others.

More About Heaven ...

The Bible tells us enough about Heaven that we know it is wonderful ...
in fact, too wonderful to imagine!
The concepts in this book were taken from the following Bible verses.

That is what is meant by the Scriptures which say
that no mere man has ever seen, heard or even imagined
what wonderful things God has ready for those who love the Lord.
I Corinthians 2:9 LB

And the material of the wall was jasper; and the city was pure gold, like clear glass.
The foundation stones of the city wall were adorned
with every kind of precious stone.... And the twelve gates were pearls;
each one of the gates was a single pearl.
And the street of the city was pure gold, like transparent glass.
Revelation 21:18-19, 21 NAS

And I heard a loud voice from the throne saying,
"Now the dwelling of God is with men, and he will live with them.
They will be his people, and God himself will be with them and be their God.
He will wipe every tear from their eyes. There will be no more death or mourning
or crying or pain, for the old order of things has passed away."
Revelation 21:3-4 NIV

And he showed me a river of the water of life, clear as crystal,
coming from the throne of God and of the Lamb, in the middle of its street.
And on either side of the river was the tree of life bearing twelve kinds of fruit,
yielding its fruit every month.... And there shall no longer be any night;
and they shall not have need of the light of a lamp nor the light of the sun,
because the Lord God shall illumine them;
and they shall reign forever and ever.
Revelation 22:1-2, 5 NAS

And they sang a new song.... Then I looked and I heard the voice of many angels around the throne, the living creatures, and the elders; and the number of them was ten thousand times ten thousand, and thousands of thousands, saying with a loud voice: "Worthy is the Lamb who was slain To receive power and riches and wisdom, And strength and honor and glory and blessing!"
Revelation 5:9, 11-12 NKJ

[Jesus] said to them, "Let the little children come to me, and do not hinder them, for the kingdom of God belongs to such as these."
Mark 10:14 NIV

Take heed that you do not despise one of these little ones, for I say to you that in heaven their angels always see the face of My Father who is in heaven.
Matthew 18:10 NKJ

Finally the beggar died and was carried by the angels to be with Abraham in the place of the righteous dead.
Luke 16:22 LB

Or take another illustration: A woman has ten valuable silver coins and loses one. Won't she light a lamp and look in every corner of the house and sweep every nook and cranny until she finds it? And then won't she call in her friends and neighbors to rejoice with her? In the same way there is joy in the presence of the angels of God when one sinner repents.
Luke 15:8-10 LB

Note: *The Lamb* is a name used for Jesus Christ.